ORIGAMI FUN
INSECTS

BY ELIZABETH NEUENFELDT

BELLWETHER MEDIA • MINNEAPOLIS, MN

This edition first published in 2021 by Bellwether Media, Inc.

No part of this publication may be reproduced in whole or in part without written permission of the publisher.
For information regarding permission, write to Bellwether Media, Inc., Attention: Permissions Department,
6012 Blue Circle Drive, Minnetonka, MN 55343.

Library of Congress Cataloging-in-Publication Data

Names: Neuenfeldt, Elizabeth, author.
Title: Origami fun: insects / Elizabeth Neuenfeldt.
Description: Minneapolis, MN : Bellwether Media, 2021. | Includes bibliographical references and index. |
    Audience: Ages 7-13 | Audience: Grades 3-8 | Summary: "Information accompanies step-by-step instructions on how to fold
    origami insects. The text level and subject matter are intended for students in grades 3 through 8"– Provided by publisher.
Identifiers: LCCN 2020003032 (print) | LCCN 2020003033 (ebook) | ISBN 9781644872956 (library binding) |
    ISBN 9781681037646 (ebook)
Subjects: LCSH: Origami–Juvenile literature. | Insects–Juvenile literature.
Classification: LCC TT872.5 .N458 2021 (print) | LCC TT872.5 (ebook) | DDC 736/.982–dc23
LC record available at https://lccn.loc.gov/2020003032
LC ebook record available at https://lccn.loc.gov/2020003033

Text copyright © 2021 by Bellwether Media, Inc. PILOT, EXPRESS, and associated logos are trademarks
and/or registered trademarks of Bellwether Media, Inc.

Editors: Sarah Eason and Christina Leaf
Designers: Paul Myerscough and Laura Sowers

Printed in the United States of America, North Mankato, MN.

TABLE OF CONTENTS

ORIGAMI FUN

Origami is the art of folding paper. It has been used for hundreds of years. Origami artists make stunning animals, buildings, and other models from a flat sheet of paper. They fold it carefully and slowly to create a work of art.

Anyone can learn the art of origami. In this book, you will learn how to make fun origami insects!

SUPPLIES
- colorful origami paper
- ruler or spoon for flattening folds
- googly eyes
- black pen
- glue
- scissors

ORIGAMI SYMBOLS
Below are key origami instruction symbols. You will find these throughout the book.

Valley fold

Mountain fold

Pleat fold

Cut line

Center line

Fold direction

Flip paper

Rotate paper

ORIGAMI FOLDS

Valley fold
Lift the paper and bend it toward you.

Mountain fold
Bend the paper backward, away from you.

Pleat fold
First fold the paper in one direction and then in the opposite direction.

Squash fold
Two layers open and are then squashed flat.

Inside reverse fold
Push the tip of the paper inward, then flatten.

Outside reverse fold
Open the paper slightly and fold the tip outward, then flatten.

Bird base fold

Squash fold   Squash fold

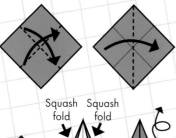

Squash fold   Squash fold

Squash fold   Squash fold

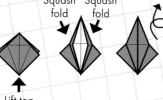

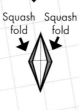

Lift top layer

Repeat

Lift top layer

Boat base fold

Lift and squash fold   Lift and squash fold

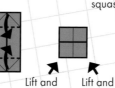
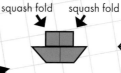

Lift and squash fold   Lift and squash fold

Fish base fold

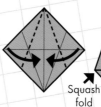
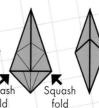

Squash fold   Squash fold

5

HONEYBEE

Paper size:
Square sheet of origami paper,
6 x 6 inches (15 x 15 centimeters)

Honeybees are small insects known for their black and yellow stripes. They make honey and live in **colonies**. A colony can have up to 80,000 bees! Most honeybees in a colony are workers or **drones**. There is only one queen bee. She is the mother of all the bees in the colony!

1

Place your paper colored-side down. Valley fold the bottom of your paper to the top.

2

Valley fold the left and right corners to the top.

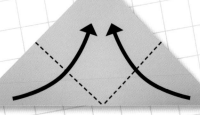

3

Valley fold down the top flaps.

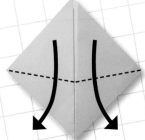

4

Valley fold down the top.

TIPS AND TRICKS

Make a soft crease in the paper. Make sure it is in the right place before you press down hard to make a sharp crease.

5

Valley fold down the top again.

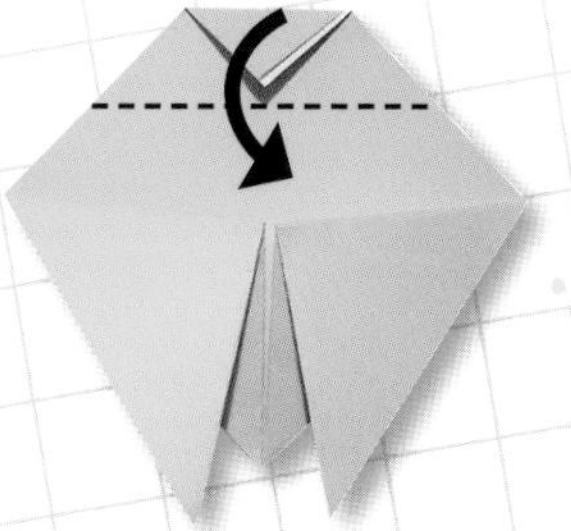

6

Valley fold down the top one more time.

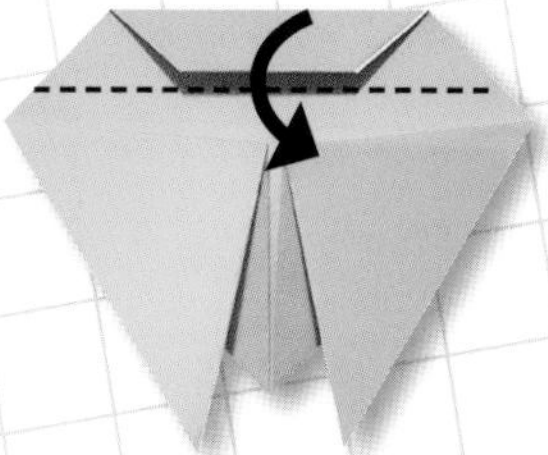

7

Mountain fold the left and right sides.

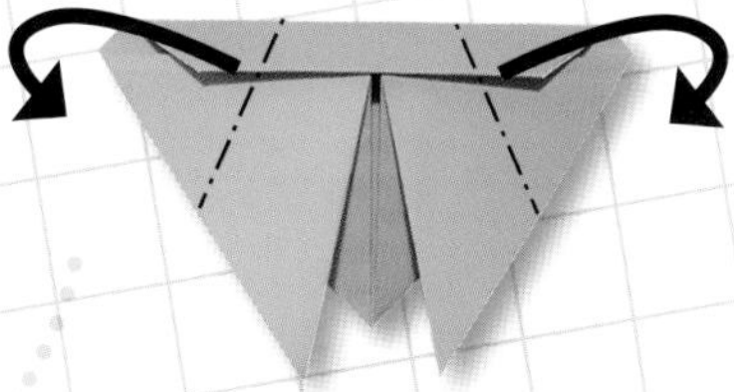

8

Cut the wings to give them a rounded shape. Then, using a black pen, add black stripes.

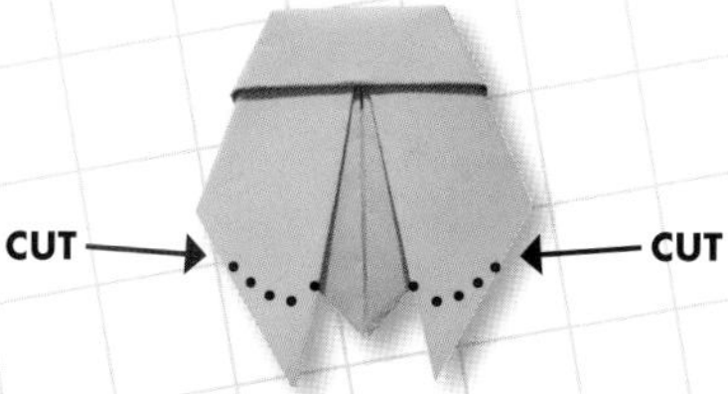

BUZZZZZ!

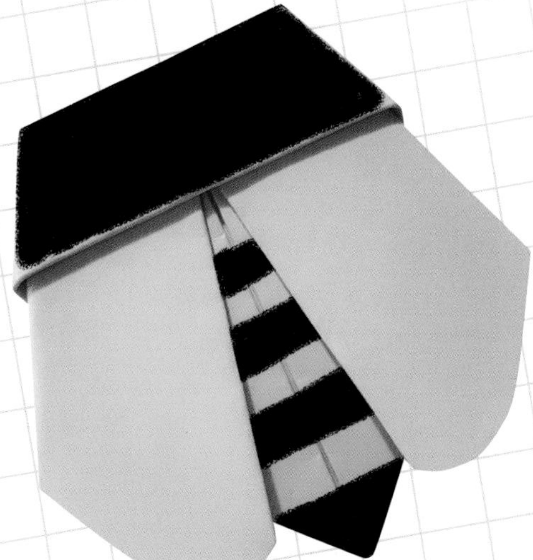

Paper size:
Square sheet of origami paper,
6 x 6 inches (15 x 15 centimeters)

Goliath beetles are insects that live in the **tropical** regions of Africa. At more than 4 inches (10 centimeters) long, they are some of the largest insects in the world! Goliath beetles have big wings, too. Their wings are larger than some birds' wings!

1

Begin with a fish base. Mountain fold back the top piece behind the model.

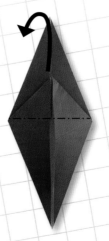

2

Valley fold the top left and right sides to the center.

3

Pleat fold the top triangle.

4

Pleat fold the top triangle again.

5

Valley fold out the top two triangles to the side.

6

Valley fold in the top two triangles to shape the pincers.

8

7

Valley fold in the sides to shape the body, squashing the folds at the top as you do so.

8

Cut the upper layer three times to create four legs, then valley fold out the legs to the sides.

CUT CUT
CUT

TIPS AND TRICKS
The pointed end of a chopstick is useful for lifting corners and edges.

9

Cut the back layer to create the last two legs and pleat fold them out to the sides.

CUT

10

Turn your model over and add some googly eyes to complete it.

PINCH, PINCH!

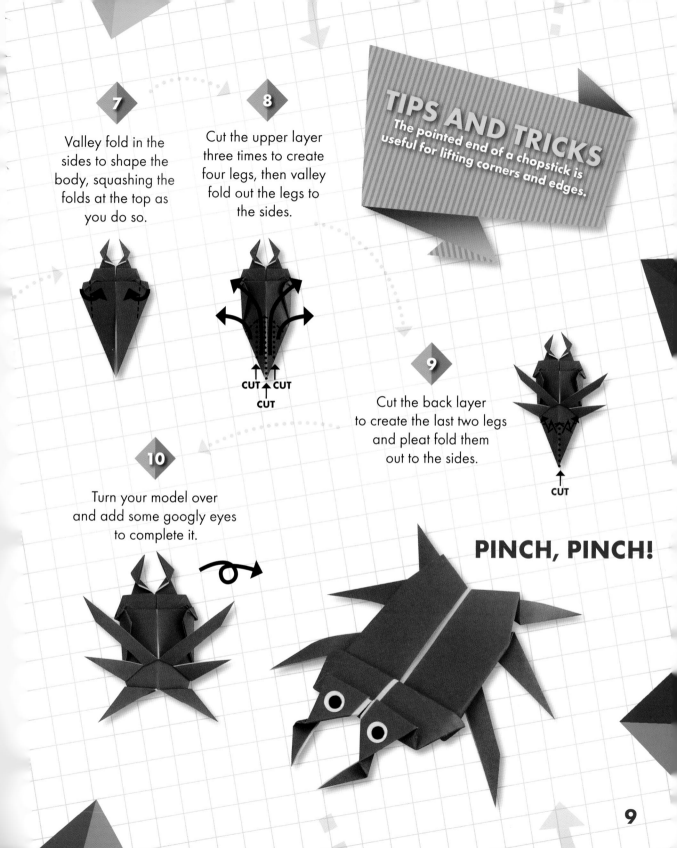

9

GRASSHOPPER

Paper size:
Square sheet of origami paper,
6 x 6 inches (15 x 15 centimeters)

Grasshoppers are powerful jumpers that come in many different colors. These insects can be green, gray, or even red! There are more than 10,000 species of grasshoppers around the world. They are found on every continent except Antarctica. In some countries, people eat roasted grasshoppers as a yummy treat!

1

Start with a bird base with the open end at the bottom. Valley fold in the sides to the center.

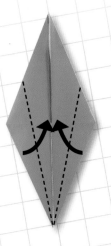

2

Valley fold down the top upper triangle.

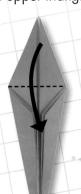

3

Mountain fold down the top lower triangle behind your model.

4

Mountain fold your model in half and rotate it 90 degrees counter-clockwise.

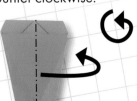

5

Gently pull up the top layer at a slight angle.

PULL

TIPS AND TRICKS

If you make a big mistake when you fold, recycle the paper and start over. A fold in the wrong place can throw your grasshopper out of balance!

6

Valley fold the upper triangle to create a leg.

7

Valley fold down the leg again to shape it.

8

Turn your model over and repeat steps 6 and 7 on the lower triangle leg. Add eyes to finish.

HOP, HOP!

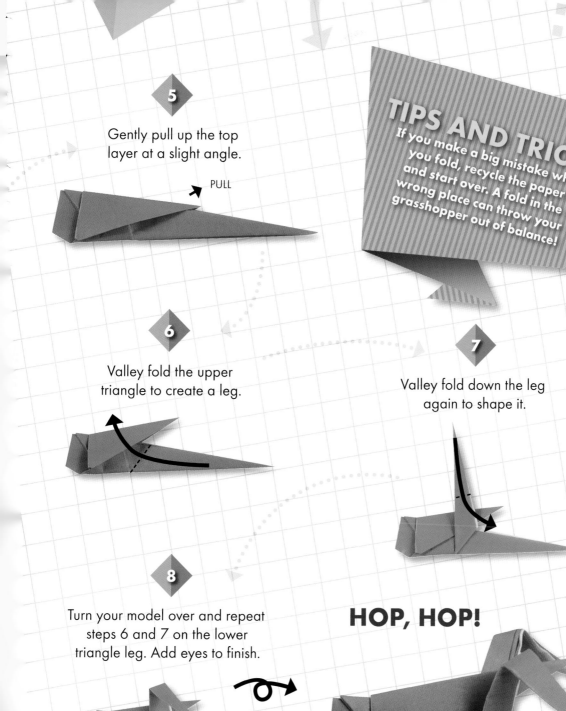

BUTTERFLY

Paper size:
Square sheet of origami paper,
6 x 6 inches (15 x 15 centimeters)

Butterflies are insects known for their large, colorful wings. There are about 17,500 species of butterflies around the world! Some butterflies, such as monarchs, fly south each fall to avoid the cold winter. They travel as far as 3,000 miles (4,828 kilometers) from Canada down to Mexico!

Start with a boat base. Mountain fold your model in half.

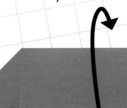

Valley fold down the top left and right layers toward the center.

Valley fold the top left and right layers toward the center again.

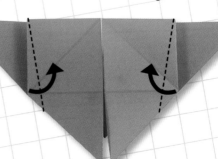

4

To shape the body, valley fold the center while mountain folding the left and right wings.

FLY AWAY!

5

Open your butterfly.

OPEN

ANT

Paper size:
2 square sheets of origami paper,
6 x 6 inches (15 x 15 centimeters)

Ants are small insects that live all around the world. They are usually no more than about 1 inch (2.54 centimeters) long. Ants may be small, but they are very strong. A single ant can carry 50 times its own body weight! They use this super strength to bring food to their colony.

1

Begin with your paper colored-side down. Valley fold your paper in half, then unfold.

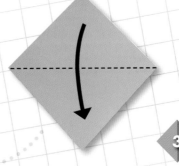

3

Valley fold the top and bottom sections in again to the center.

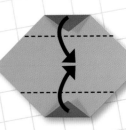

2

Valley fold the top and bottom triangles in.

5

Make an outside reverse fold to the right side.

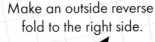

4

Valley fold the top down.

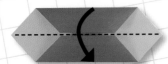

6
Make another outside
reverse fold to the right side.

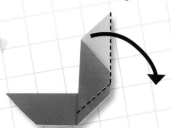

7
Make an outside reverse fold
to the left side.

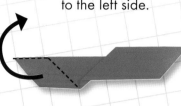

8
Make another outside
reverse fold to the left side.

9
Mountain fold the
bottom upper layer and
tuck inside model.
Repeat on the reverse side.

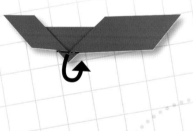

10
Inside reverse fold the left
and right sides to shape
the head and body.

11
Your model should now look
like this. Put to one side. Take
another piece of paper and
cut into three strips.

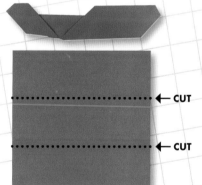

← CUT

← CUT

12
Repeatedly valley fold
the strips up into legs.

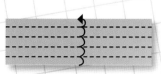

13
Shape the legs using valley
and mountain folds, then
place your model on top.
Use glue to secure it
in place if needed.
Add eyes to finish.

READY TO WORK!

DRAGONFLY

Paper size:
Square sheet of origami paper,
6 x 6 inches (15 x 15 centimeters)

Dragonflies are flying insects with big wings. Their **wingspans** are between 2 and 5 inches (5 and 13 centimeters) wide. Dragonflies can move each of their four wings independently. This makes them skilled fliers. They can fly forward, backward, and straight up or down. They can even **hover**!

1

Start with a bird base with the open end at the bottom. Mountain fold down the top back flap.

2

Pull the bottom front flaps out to the sides, opening them up as you do. Lift the top triangle slightly and tuck the bottom flap in behind, then squash the flap.

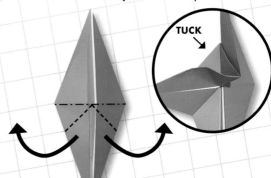

TUCK

3

Valley fold the sides of the top flap in to the center, squashing down the folds at the same time.

4

Your model should look like this. Turn it over.

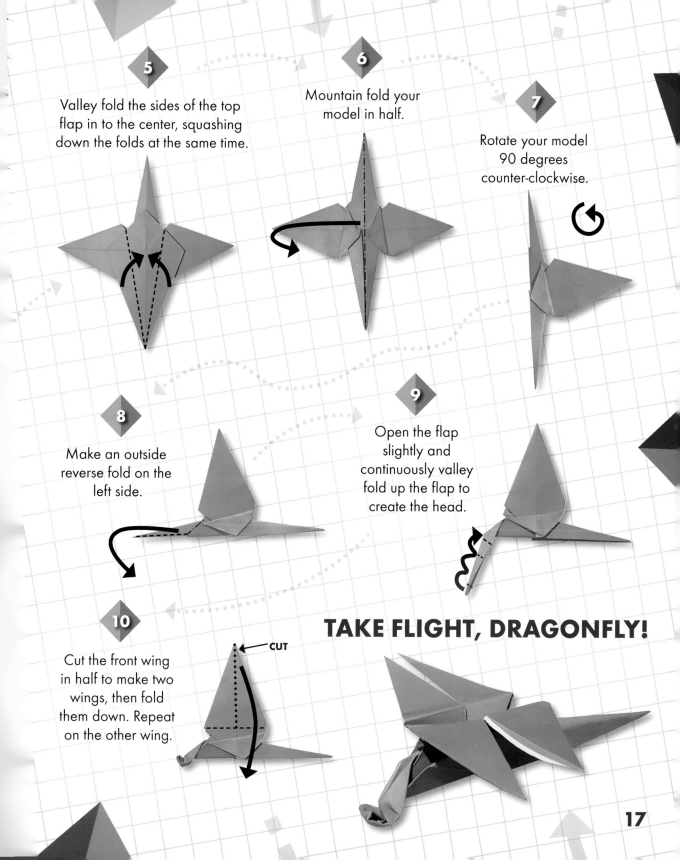

5

Valley fold the sides of the top flap in to the center, squashing down the folds at the same time.

6

Mountain fold your model in half.

7

Rotate your model 90 degrees counter-clockwise.

8

Make an outside reverse fold on the left side.

9

Open the flap slightly and continuously valley fold up the flap to create the head.

10

Cut the front wing in half to make two wings, then fold them down. Repeat on the other wing.

CUT

TAKE FLIGHT, DRAGONFLY!

WALKINGSTICK

Paper size:
2 square sheets of origami paper,
6 x 6 inches (15 x 15 centimeters)

Walkingsticks, or stick insects, look exactly like their name! Their color and stick-like bodies allow them to blend in with plants and trees. This helps stick insects hide from **predators**! Walkingsticks come in many sizes. The largest grow to be 2 feet (64 centimeters) long!

1

Valley fold the bottom corner of your sheet of paper to the top corner.

2

Take a very small section at the bottom and valley fold it up.

3

Cut the ends to create the antennae. Then fold the bottom flaps in to shape the head.

CUT→

4

Repeatedly valley fold the bottom up all the way to the top. You have now created the body.

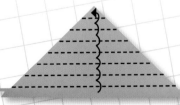

5

Your model should look like this. Put to one side.

6

Cut another piece of paper into three pieces.

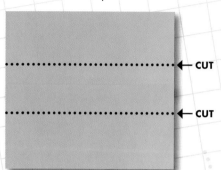

← CUT

← CUT

7

Repeatedly valley fold the pieces to create the legs.

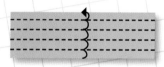

8

Valley fold and mountain fold the sides of each leg to give them shape.

9

Place the body on top of the legs. You can use a bit of glue to help keep them in place. Add eyes to finish.

TRY TO FIND ME!

Paper size:
Square sheet of origami paper,
6 x 6 inches (15 x 15 centimeters)

Praying mantises are deadly **carnivores**. While hunting for food, these insects stay very still and put their front legs together like they are praying. When **prey** is near, they quickly strike with their front legs. Praying mantises eat spiders, insects, frogs, lizards, and mice. Some even eat other praying mantises!

1

Start with a bird base with the open end at the bottom. Valley fold both the upper and lower left and right sides in to the center.

2

Valley fold the top upper layer down.

3

Your model should look like this. Turn your model over.

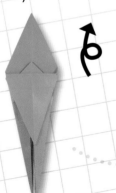

4

Cut the bottom triangle along the dotted lines. Valley fold the three upper triangle layers. These will create the "praying arms."

CUT

5

Pleat fold the arms at the ends to create the praying hands.

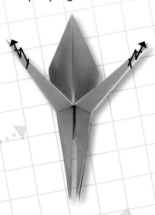

20

6

Mountain fold the next triangle layer to shape the back legs.

7

Mountain fold the next triangle layer to shape the front legs.

8

Mountain fold the front legs again to shape them.

9

Valley fold your model in half.

10

Make a squash fold to create the head.

SQUASH FOLD

11

Mountain fold and tuck the point of the head. Rotate your model slightly so the legs are parallel to the ground. Add eyes to finish.

ON THE HUNT!

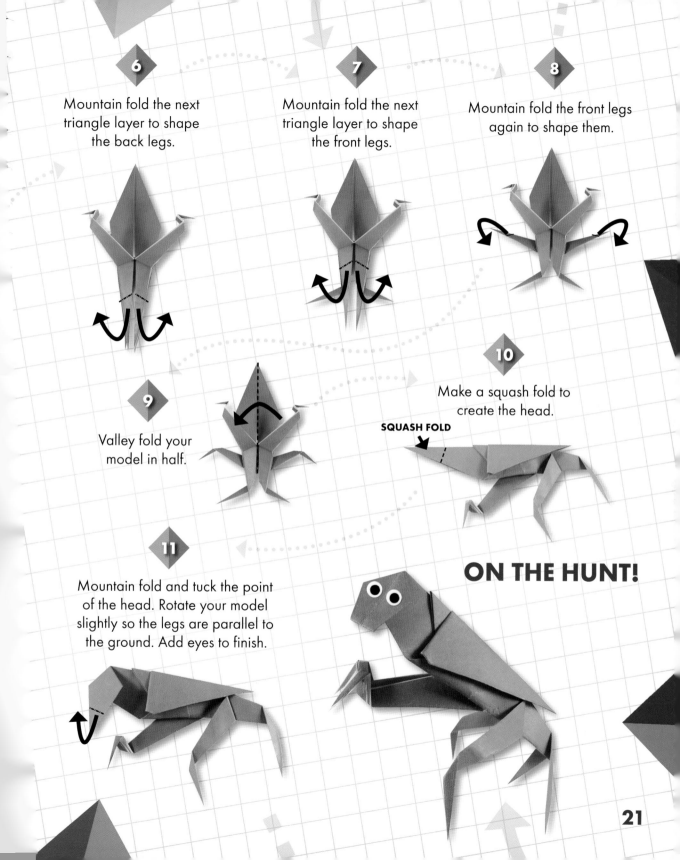

GLOSSARY

carnivores—animals or insects that only eat meat

colonies—groups of a species that live together in the same area

drones—male bees in a colony

hover—to stay in one spot while in flight

predators—animals that hunt other animals for food

prey—animals that are hunted by other animals for food

species—types of an animal that share the same traits; the monarch butterfly is a species of butterfly.

tropical—related to the tropics; the tropics is a hot region near the equator.

wingspans—measurements of the distance between the tip of one wing to the tip of the other wing

TO LEARN MORE

AT THE LIBRARY

Forest, Christopher. *Beehives.* Lake Elmo, Minn.: Focus Readers, 2019.

Mills, Andrea. *Bugs.* New York, N.Y.: DK Publishing, 2017.

Romero, Libby. *Insects.* Washington, D.C.: National Geographic, 2017.

ON THE WEB

FACTSURFER

Factsurfer.com gives you a safe, fun way to find more information.

1. Go to www.factsurfer.com.

2. Enter "insect origami" into the search box and click 🔍.

3. Select your book cover to see a list of related content.

INDEX